"All right, leave it to us!"

"Please make a very good one."

Who Made This Cake?

TEXT AND ENGLISH TRANSLATION BY **Chihiro Nakagawa**   ILLUSTRATIONS BY **Junji Koyose**

FRONT STREET
HONESDALE, PENNSYLVANIA

Here we go!

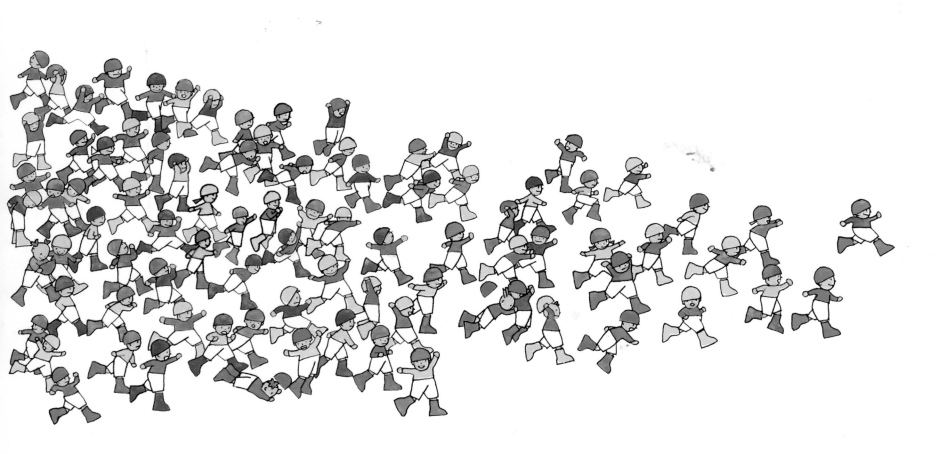

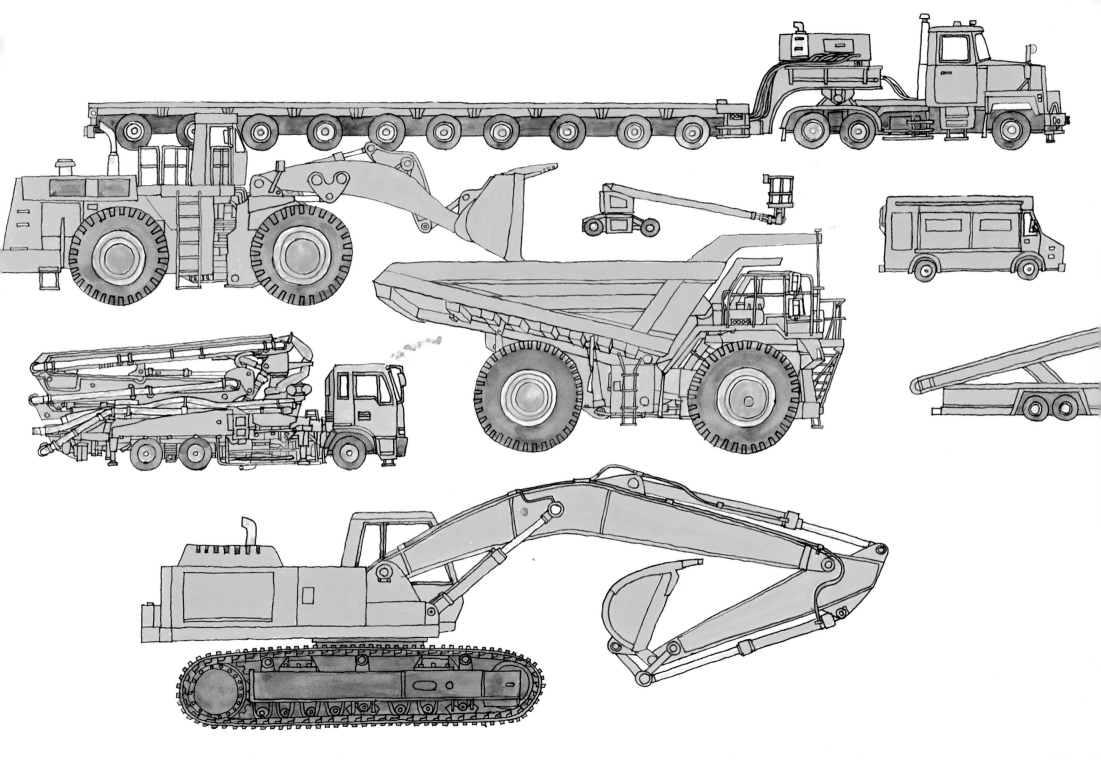

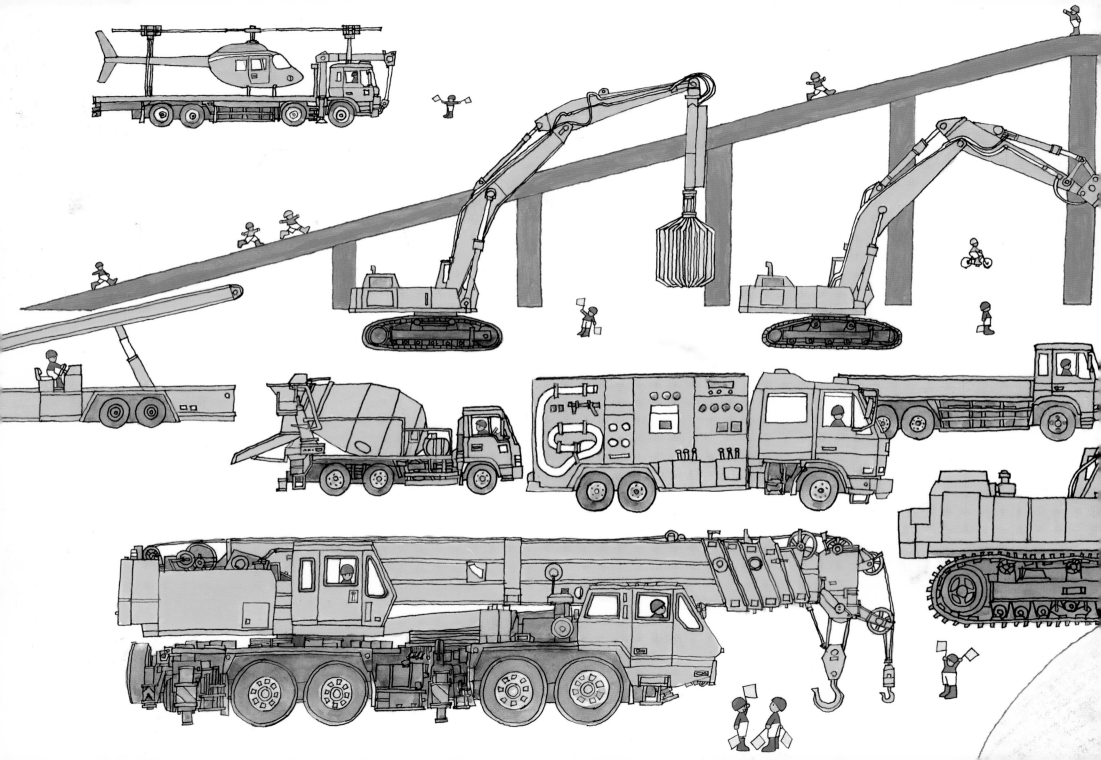

Eggs and butter, flour, sugar, and baking powder.

Look what our construction vehicles can do.

Any kind of job, you can rely on us.

Mix it well.

GRRRRRRRRRRRRRRR...

Pour the mixture in a pan.

Load it in the oven.

Press the button, and let's take a break.

It's done!

Mmmm, it smells good!

Put the whipped cream on …

and spread it neatly.

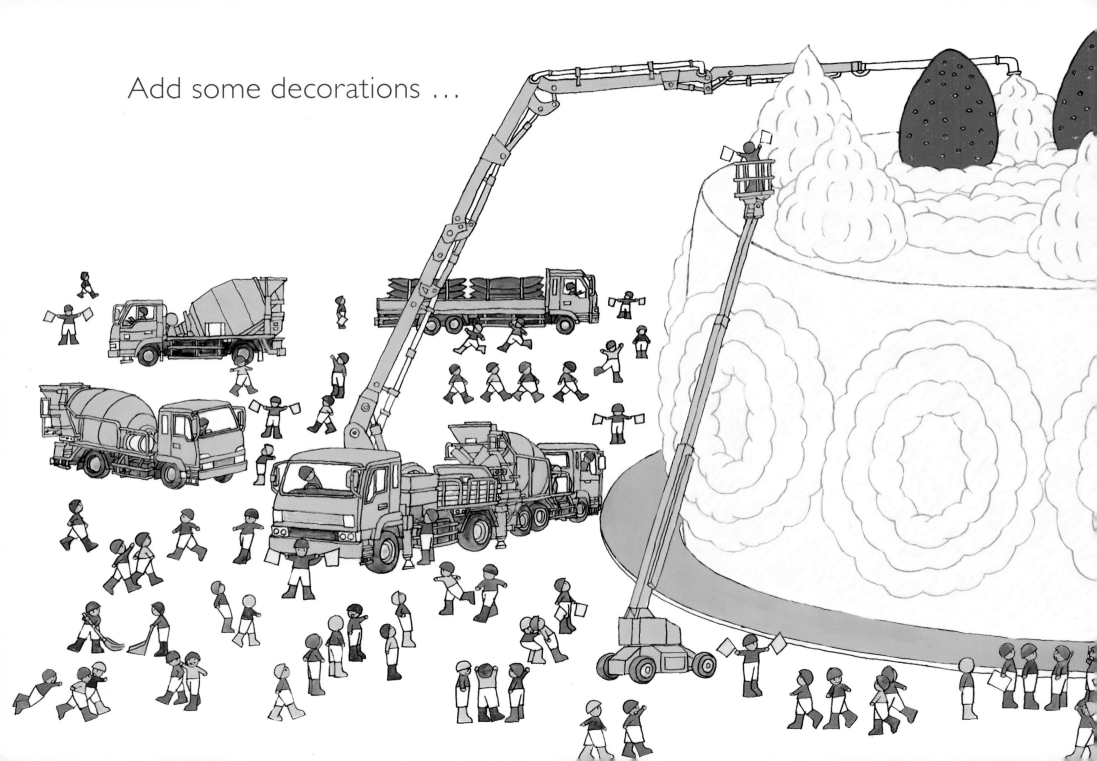

Add some decorations …

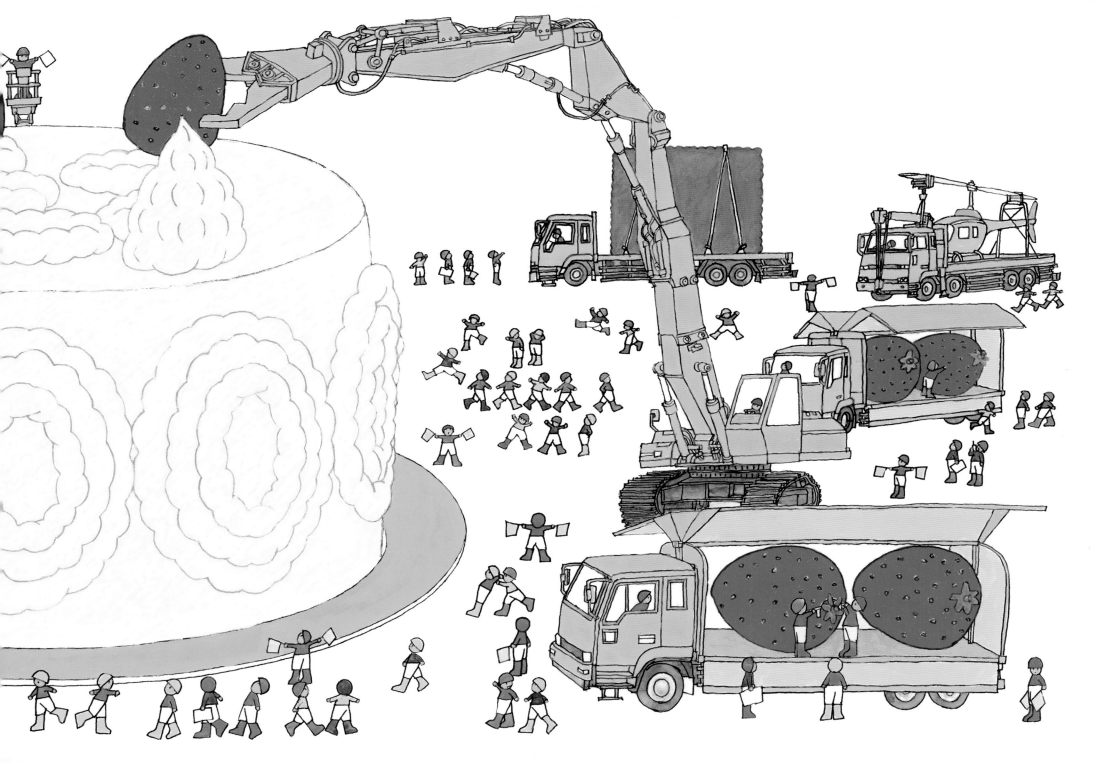

and the finishing touch …

The job is done!

First published in Japan in 2007 by Tokuma Shoten Publishing Co., Ltd.
English translation rights arranged with Tokuma Shoten Publishing Co., Ltd., through Japan Foreign-Rights Centre.

Printed in China
First U.S. edition, 2008
Fourth printing

Nakagawa, Chihiro.
Who made this cake? / Chihiro Nakagawa ; illustrations by Junji Koyose ; English text by Chihiro Nakagawa. — 1st ed.
p. cm.
ISBN 978-1-59078-595-9 (hardcover : alk. paper)
[1. Construction equipment—Fiction. 2. Cake—Fiction 3. Baking—Fiction. 4. Size—Fiction.] I. Koyose, Junji, ill. II. Title.
PZ7.N1399Wh 2008
[E]—dc22
2008003070

FRONT STREET
An Imprint of Boyds Mills Press, Inc.
815 Church Street
Honesdale, Pennsylvania 18431